For Desmond, "by the way" —SB

For Alek and Kyle —DS

ABOUT THIS BOOK

The illustrations for this book were done in Adobe Photoshop. This book was edited by Andrea "Full Moon-er" Spooner and designed by David "Skullcaplan" Caplan and Kelly "Kelleeeeeeeek!" Brennan. The production was supervised by Nyamekye "WaliyayaAAAAAAH!" Waliyaya, and the production editor was Andy "Costume" Ball. The text was set in DanSantat, and the display type is hand-lettered.

Text copyright © 2021 by Samantha Berger • Illustrations copyright © 2021 by Dan Santat • Cover illustration copyright © 2021 by Dan Santat • Cover design by David Caplan • Cover copyright © 2021 by Hachette Book Group, Inc. • Hachette Book Group supports the right to free expression and the value of copyright. The purpose of copyright is to encourage writers and artists to produce the creative works that enrich our culture. • The scanning, uploading, and distribution of this book without permission is a theft of the author's intellectual property. If you would like permission to use material from the book (other than for review purposes), please contact permissions@hbgusa.com. Thank you for your support of the author's rights. • Little, Brown and Company • Hachette Book Group • 1290 Avenue of the Americas, New York, NY 10104 • Visit us at LBYR.com • First Edition: July 2021 • Little, Brown and Company is a division of Hachette Book Group, Inc. • The Little, Brown name and logo are trademarks of Hachette Book Group, Inc. • The publisher is not responsible for websites (or their content) that are not owned by the publisher. • Library of Congress Cataloging-in-Publication Data • Names: Berger, Samantha, author. • Santat, Dan, illustrator. • Title: Trick or treat, Crankenstein / written by Samantha Berger ; illustrated by Dan Santat. • Description: First edition. • New York : Little, Brown and Company, 2021. • Audience: Ages 4–8. • Audience: Grades K–1. • Summary: A boy who looks ordinary transforms into grumbling Crankenstein when he receives more tricks than treats on Halloween. • Identifiers: LCCN 2020023282 (print) • Subjects: CYAC: Halloween—Fiction. • Monsters—Fiction. • Classification: LCC PZ7.B452136 Tr 2021 (print) • DDC [E]—dc23 • LC record available at https://lccn.loc.gov/2020023282 • ISBN: 978-0-316-45809-2 (hardcover) • PRINTED IN CHINA • APS • 10 9 8 7 6 5 4 3 2 1

TRICK OR TREAT, CRANKENSTEIN

Written by SAMANTHA BERGER

Illustrated by DAN SANTAT

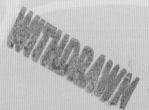

L B

LITTLE, BROWN AND COMPANY
NEW YORK · BOSTON

Do you know what today is?
Crankenstein knows what today is.
It's a day that rhymes with Schmalloween, and
it's Crankenstein's FAVORITE day of the year.

EXCEPT—when he wakes up with a toothache, which makes eating Ghosty-O's cereal extra challenging.

Crankenstein would say,

EXCEPT—when his brother doesn't know WHAT he's supposed to be, and laughs till he falls off the couch.

Crankenstein would say,

MEHHRRRR!

EXCEPT—when a storm suddenly blows in JUST as he's leaving for the Big Fall Festival...

and his costume isn't exactly waterproof.

This is a day where you might find
Crankenstein lost in a corn maze...

Or carving a pumpkin, which is...
NOT. GOING. AS PLANNED.

Or standing next to someone wearing the EXACT same thing in the costume parade...

ONLY SO. MUCH. BETTER.

You can be sure to spot Crankenstein trick-or-treating at the house that gives out toothbrushes instead of candy.

Crankenstein

CAN'T

STAND

that!

MOUTH STRING

Or when he's startled by a big, boingy spider. Crankenstein DOES NOT CARE for big, boingy spiders!

And you'll *definitely* see Crankenstein when his brother sneaks candy from his stash.

Crankenstein DID NOT SIGN OFF on his brother sneaking candy from his stash!

This is NOT what Crankenstein had in mind for his favorite holiday of the year.

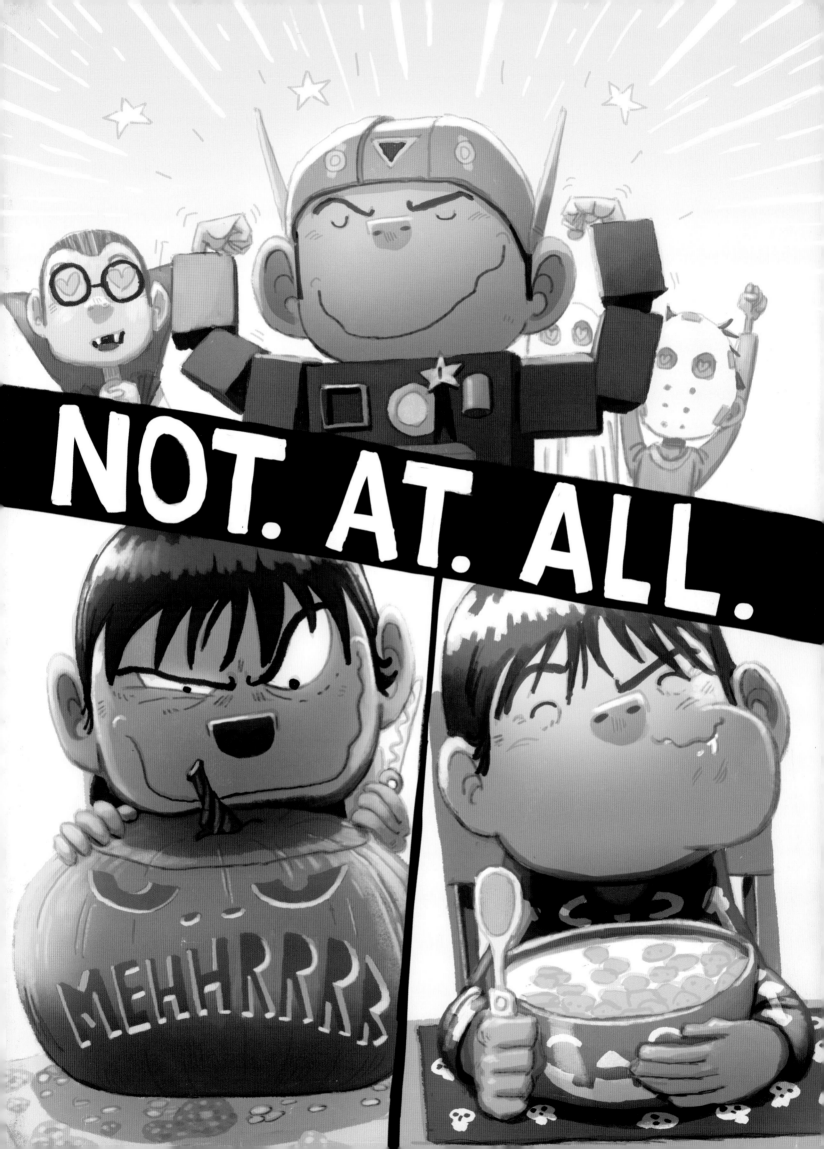

But just when you're sure Crankenstein has never had a crankier Halloween, someone might come to the door who looks a little familiar.

BING BONG!

MEHR?

And when Crankenstein sees someone dressed up as Crankenstein for Halloween...

Because nothing is as funny
as seeing yourself so cranky.

EXCEPT...

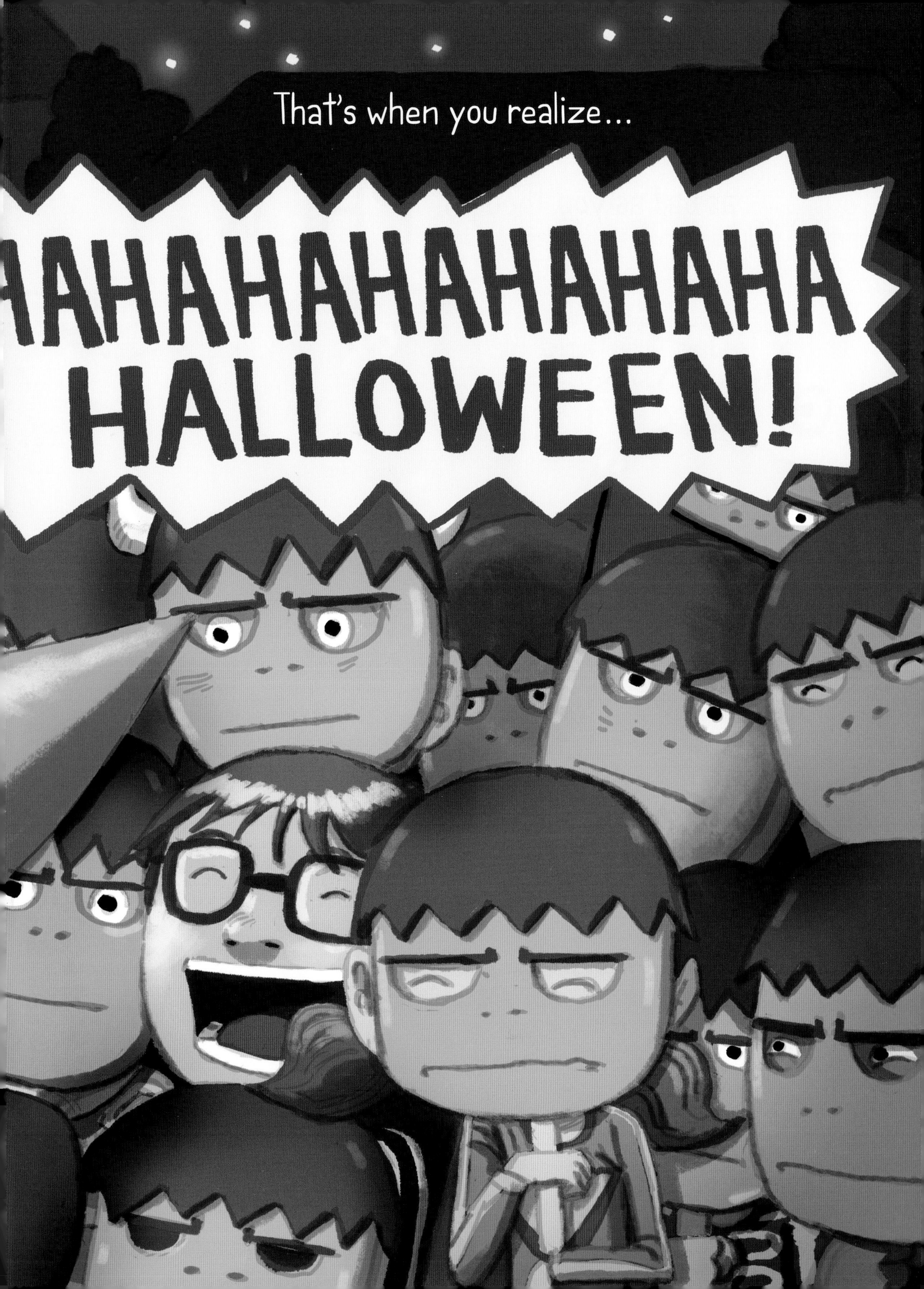
That's when you realize...
AHAHAHAHAHAHAHAHA
HALLOWEEN!

...this Halloween might not be QUITE as bad as you thought. PHEW.

31901066823511